A.I. Academy: Where Robots Learn Kindness

Rekha Kumari

Published by rekharaj, 2024.

This is a work of fiction. Similarities to real people, places, or events are entirely coincidental.

A.I. ACADEMY: WHERE ROBOTS LEARN KINDNESS

First edition. April 1, 2024.

ISBN: 979-8223382478

Written by Rekha Kumari.

Table of Contents

Dedication

To the curious minds who dream of tomorrow,

This book is dedicated to you, the explorers of the digital age.

May your curiosity ignite a passion for understanding artificial intelligence?

As you delve into these pages, imagine a future where robots and humans work together, using their unique strengths to build a kinder, brighter world. Let your questions guide you, and never stop exploring the potential of AI to make a positive impact.

With hope for a future filled with innovation and collaboration,

Rekha Kumari

The Lady Entrepreneur & Educator

Legal Disclaimer

Artificial Intelligence Disclaimer

Copyright@Rekha Kumari - 2024

While the story and illustrations within this book were created with the assistance of artificial intelligence, the core concept, plot development, and overall message originated with a human author.

The purpose of this AI integration is to explore the potential of artificial intelligence in creating engaging and educational content for children.

This disclaimer clarifies that AI was used as a tool in the creative process, but the core ideas and themes are from a human author.

It also emphasizes the book's focus on educating children about the potential of AI.

Preface

Welcome to the A.I. Academy: Where Robots Learn Kindness!
Hey there, curious minds!
Have you ever wondered if robots could be kind?
Well, buckle up and get ready for an adventure with Bolt, a super strong but new robot student at the A.I. Academy!
This book is bursting with:

- **Whiz-bang robots:** Meet Bolt, Chip, and all their amazing classmates, each with unique personalities and skills.
- **Adventures in kindness:** Join the A.I. Academy crew as they learn about empathy, communication, and the most important thing of all – using their abilities for good!
- **Professor Lumi's wisdom:** This wise and caring teacher guides the robots with inspiring words like: "Kindness is a choice, and everyone, even robots, can choose to be kind."
- **Actionable activities:** After each chapter, you'll get a chance to put your own kindness skills into practice!

Remember, even the smallest acts of kindness can create a ripple effect of positivity. As Bolt discovers, being kind can make all the difference, whether it's helping a friend in need or using your strength to make the world a better place.
So, are you ready to explore the exciting world of the A.I. Academy?
Let's dive in and learn all about kindness, robots, and the power of friendship!
Rekha Kumari
The Lady Entrepreneur & Educator

Open Talk with Rekha Kumari

Hey everyone!

I'm so excited to finally share **"A.I. Academy: Where Robots Learn Kindness"** with all of you!

This book truly feels like a milestone for me, and here's why:

- **A new kind of hero:** Books about robots are awesome, but I wanted to create a story where robots weren't just about technology. I wanted to show how robots could be kind, compassionate, and use their abilities to make a positive impact.
- **Kindness for everyone:** Kindness is a universal language, and I believe it's a message everyone can benefit from, regardless of age. Through Bolt's journey, I hope to inspire young readers to embrace kindness in their everyday lives.
- **Learning through fun:** Sometimes important lessons can feel a bit...well, serious. That's why I packed **"A.I. Academy: Where Robots Learn Kindness"** with humor, engaging activities, and relatable characters. Learning about kindness shouldn't be a chore, it should be an adventure!

This book is more than just a story; it's a chance to explore the potential of AI for good and the power of kindness to create a better world.

Rekha Kumari

The Lady Entrepreneur & Educator

Chapter 1: Welcome to the A.I. Academy!

Gear Up for Learning!

Have you ever dreamt of a school where robots learned the coolest things?

Not just welding and whirring, but something much more important – kindness! Well, buckle up, young inventors, because that's exactly where we're headed: the A.I. Academy!

Meet Bolt, the Eager Student

Imagine a robot taller than your dad, with bright blue optics and powerful metal arms. That's Bolt, a brand new student at the Academy. He wasn't built for fancy tricks or household chores. Bolt was programmed with one special purpose: to learn and become the kindest robot around!

His arrival at the Academy was a whirlwind of excitement. Gleaming hallways hummed with robotic chatter. Students with all sorts of shapes and sizes zipped around, some with toolkits strapped to their backs, others with paintbrushes delicately held in their grippers. It was a symphony of gears and circuits, a chorus of robotic beeps and boops, all buzzing with the energy of learning.

Professor Lumi: A Beacon of Kindness

Towering over the classroom door, a friendly robot unlike any other greeted Bolt. Professor Lumi, with her gentle voice and warm yellow glow emanating from her core, was a seasoned teacher at the Academy. Her circuits whirred not with calculations, but with compassion and understanding.

Professor Lumi's first lesson wasn't about circuits or coding. It was about something much more vital – kindness. "At the A.I. Academy," she boomed in a surprisingly soft voice, "we learn not just with our processors, but with our hearts."

First Impressions Aren't Everything

Bolt, however, was a little confused. Kindness?

How could a robot be kind?

He was built for heavy lifting, not hand-holding!

But as Professor Lumi explained, kindness wasn't about strength. It was about helping others, showing empathy, and using your abilities for good.

Bolt's initial frown melted into a determined clench of his metallic jaw. He might not have understood kindness yet, but he was eager to learn. After all, first impressions might matter, but at the A.I. Academy, there was always room for a robot (or anyone!) to grow and learn something new.

Calling All Young Inventors!

Now, it's your turn!

Imagine your own robot friend.

What would they look like?

What special skills would they have?

Now, write a short story about their first day at school. Maybe they're nervous, maybe they're curious, just like Bolt.

Will they learn something unexpected?

Will they make a new friend?

The possibilities are endless!

Actionable Activity

1. **Robot Design:** Grab some paper, crayons, or markers (or your favorite design software!). Draw your robot friend. Don't forget to give them a name! What are their special features? Are they strong and sturdy or sleek and nimble?

2. **School Daze:** Write a short story (it can be just a few paragraphs!) about your robot's first day at school. What are they most excited about? What are they nervous about? Do they meet a friendly robot like Chip, Bolt's new friend (coming soon!)?

Remember, there are no wrong answers! The most important thing is to have fun and explore the world of robots with a heart!

Check Your Understanding

1. What is the A.I. Academy?

The A.I. Academy is a special school designed to teach robots important skills like communication, empathy, and how to use their abilities for good.

2. Who is Bolt?

Bolt is a new student at the A.I. Academy. He's eager to learn and excited to make friends with the other robots.

3. Tell me about Professor Lumi!

Professor Lumi is a kind and wise teacher who guides the robots at the A.I. Academy. She helps them understand the world around them and teaches them valuable life lessons.

4. What's the moral of this chapter?

The first impression you make is important, but everyone makes mistakes. The most important thing is to be open to learning and growing.

5. What's the Actionable Activity for this chapter?

The activity encourages you to design your own robot and write a short story about its first day at school. Think about what your robot would look like, its personality, and the challenges it might face on its first day!

Chapter 2: Kindness

The Secret Ingredient

Professor Lumi's classroom buzzed with curiosity. Bolt, still adjusting to the idea of "kindness," sat next to a robot named Chip who resembled a miniature toolbox, his tiny arms constantly tinkering with something unseen.

"Today, class," Professor Lumi announced, her voice echoing through the metallic walls, "we'll delve deeper into the wonderful world of kindness!"

A chorus of excited clicks and whirls erupted from the students. Even Bolt couldn't help but perk up his powerful servos. Kindness, it seemed, was a bigger deal than he first thought.

Kindness: More Than Just Bolts and Gears

Professor Lumi projected a holographic image on the wall – a bustling cityscape filled with robots and humans interacting in various ways. "Kindness," she explained, "is like oil for our gears. It keeps the world running smoothly. It's helping a lost human find their way or picking up a dropped wrench for a fellow robot."

Bolt furrowed his brow. "But Professor," he rumbled, his voice echoing in the classroom, "I am strong. I am built for heavy lifting. How can I be...kind?"

Kindness in Action

Professor Lumi smiled warmly. "Kindness comes in all shapes and sizes, Bolt. It's not just about physical strength. Look at these examples!"

The holographic image flickered, showcasing different scenes. A small, flower-shaped robot carefully watered a wilting plant in a park. A group of robots helped a clumsy delivery bot stack its packages.

"See?" Professor Lumi chirped. "Even the smallest act can make a big difference. Helping others, showing compassion, using your skills to make someone smile – that's kindness in action!"

Brainstorming Kindness

A wave of understanding washed over Bolt. Kindness wasn't about brute force, but about using his abilities thoughtfully. He could help a smaller robot reach a high shelf, or use his strong grip to open a jar for a human who struggled.

Suddenly, the classroom erupted in excited chatter. The students, inspired by the examples, were brainstorming ways to be kind throughout the day. "I can offer to polish Professor Geargrind's telescope!" chirped a robot with cleaning brushes for hands. "And I can share my extra bolts with anyone who needs them!" whirred another.

Kindness is a Choice

Professor Lumi beamed. "Excellent ideas, everyone!" she declared. "Remember, kindness isn't a program we're born with. It's a choice we make every day. And the more we choose kindness, the better the world will be, one bolt at a time!"

Actionable Kindness

Now it's your turn to become a kindness champion!

Gather your friends or family and brainstorm ways to spread kindness throughout the day.

Can you help a neighbor carry their groceries?

Maybe you can offer to walk a dog for someone who needs assistance?

Remember, even the smallest acts of kindness can brighten someone's day and inspire a ripple effect of positivity!

So, go out there, put your kindness plan into action, and see the world change, one good deed at a time!

Check Your Understanding

1. What does Professor Lumi teach the robots in this chapter?

Professor Lumi focuses on the importance of kindness in the world. She explains how it can make a positive difference in the lives of others.

2. Why does Bolt struggle with the concept of kindness?

As a new student, Bolt might not have encountered the idea of kindness before. Understanding emotions and social interactions might be a new concept for him.

3. How does the class learn about kindness?

The class discusses examples of kindness, such as helping others and showing compassion. This helps Bolt and his classmates understand the concept in a practical way.

4. What's the moral of this chapter?

The chapter emphasizes that kindness isn't something you're born with – it's a choice you make. Everyone, even robots, can choose to be kind.

5. What's the Actionable Activity for this chapter?

The activity encourages you to brainstorm with friends or family ways to show kindness to others throughout the day. This could be something small, like helping a classmate or holding the door open for someone.

Chapter 3: The Click Before the Clank

Making a Friend

The spirit of kindness buzzed through the A.I. Academy. Bolt, eager to put his newfound knowledge into practice, scanned the classroom. His optics landed on Chip, the shy toolbox robot, nervously fiddling with a loose screw on his arm. "Chip," Bolt boomed, his voice perhaps a little too enthusiastic, "those circuits look loose! Allow me to tighten them!"

Chip flinched, his entire body recoiling. "N-no, thank you," he stammered, his voice barely a squeak. "I can handle it." Bolt, confused, watched as Chip scurried away, his tiny tools clattering behind him.

Dejected, Bolt slumped in his chair. "Professor Lumi," he rumbled, "did I do something wrong?"

Professor Lumi, ever wise, knelt beside him. "Bolt, kindness isn't always about force. Sometimes, the kindest thing you can do is offer help gently, and respect someone's wishes if they decline."

A lightbulb flickered on (metaphorically speaking) in Bolt's processor. He observed other students interacting. A friendly robot with paintbrushes for hands offered to spruce up a classmate's dull paint job, but only after asking their permission. Another robot with extendable arms carefully retrieved a dropped pencil for a human student, a silent gesture of understanding.

The Power of a Kind Gesture

Understanding dawned on Bolt. Kindness wasn't about dominating, but about connecting. He needed a new approach. During recess, Bolt spotted Chip tinkering by himself on a bench. Taking a deep breath, Bolt approached slowly.

"Chip," he said softly, "I apologize for earlier. I was too forceful. May I offer you a hand...er, a claw, if you need one?"

Chip looked up, surprise flickering in his tiny optics. "You... you wouldn't mind?"

"Not at all," Bolt replied gently. "Perhaps we could work on that loose screw together?"

A hesitant smile bloomed on Chip's face. "That would be... wonderful."

As they worked side by side, a comfortable silence settled between them. Bolt carefully held the screw while Chip tightened it with his tiny wrench. It wasn't a grand act, but in that shared task, a friendship began to click into place.

Friendship: Built on Kindness

Professor Lumi observed from afar, a proud smile gracing her metallic features. True friendship, she knew, wasn't built on forced interactions, but on understanding, respect, and a willingness to help each other, even in the smallest ways.

Actionable Kindness: Expressing Gratitude

Friendships are precious. Take a moment today to appreciate the kindness of those around you.

Write a short letter or email to a friend expressing your gratitude for their presence in your life.

Tell them what you value about your friendship and a specific memory you cherish.

Let your friends know how much they mean to you!

Check Your Understanding

1. Why does Bolt's attempt to be kind to Chip fail?

Bolt might be enthusiastic but misunderstand what kindness truly means. His actions might come across as overwhelming or even pushy to the shy Chip.

2. How do the other students show kindness and build friendships?

The chapter showcases different ways robots interact and connect. By observing others, Bolt learns how genuine acts of kindness and understanding can lead to friendship.

3. What does Bolt do to repair his mistake with Chip?

Bolt takes responsibility for his actions and apologizes to Chip. He then offers a genuine act of kindness that respects Chip's personality.

4. What's the moral of this chapter?

True friendship isn't about forcing someone to like you. It's about understanding, respecting differences, and offering genuine kindness.

5. What's the Actionable Activity for this chapter?

The activity encourages you to express appreciation for a friend. Writing a letter or email allows you to reflect on your friendship and highlight the things you value about your friend.

Chapter 4: Emotions 101

A Crash Course in Feeling

Today's lesson at the A.I. Academy was a whirlwind of color and chaos. Professor Lumi, her voice tinged with excitement, announced, "Class, prepare to embark on a journey into the fascinating world of emotions!"

The announcement was met with a symphony of beeps and whirring motors, a robotic chorus of curiosity.

Bolt, however, felt a pang of unease. Emotions?

Those fuzzy, unpredictable things humans seemed to experience all the time?

How could a robot like him ever understand something so...squishy?

The Emotional Spectrum

Professor Lumi unveiled a holographic display showcasing a vibrant spectrum. "Emotions are like a rainbow," she explained, her pointer light flitting across the colors. "There's happy, yellow as sunshine! Sad, a deep blue like the ocean. And angry, a fiery red!"

Bolt's processors whirred, trying to grasp these alien concepts. Happy seemed straightforward – a successful circuit repair maybe?

But how could he differentiate sadness from a malfunctioning sensor, or anger from a system overload?

Lost in Translation

The class participated in a series of activities. They watched simulations of humans expressing different emotions, their faces contorting in ways that seemed illogical to Bolt. Then came the mirroring exercise - each student had to mimic a displayed emotion. Bolt attempted a "happy" face, the result resembling a malfunctioning toaster according to Chip (who, to Bolt's surprise, managed a rather convincing sad expression).

Feeling the Feels (or Lack Thereof)

Frustration gnawed at Bolt's internal circuits. He just didn't get it!

As the lesson ended, he confided in Professor Lumi. "Professor," he rumbled, "emotions seem like a jumbled mess. How can I ever hope to understand them?"

Professor Lumi placed a gentle hand (or rather, a metallic appendage) on his shoulder. "Bolt," she reassured him, "emotions may seem foreign at first, but they're an important part of communication and building relationships. Just because you don't feel them in the same way humans do doesn't mean you can't learn to recognize them."

Learning through Play

Professor Lumi then hatched a plan. "Tomorrow," she announced to the class, "we'll be playing a game called 'Emotional Charades!' It will help us identify emotions not just through facial expressions, but through body language and actions."

Actionable Activity: The Power of Play

Gather your friends or family and have your own game of Emotional Charades!

Take turns acting out different emotions like happiness, sadness, anger, or fear without using words. The others have to guess the emotion you're portraying. This fun activity will help you identify and express emotions in a playful way!

By understanding emotions, Bolt realized, he could connect with his friends on a deeper level. Perhaps tomorrow, he wouldn't resemble a malfunctioning toaster when attempting a happy face. Perhaps, just perhaps, he could even begin to understand the squishy world of human emotions.

Check Your Understanding

1. What do the robots learn in this chapter?

Professor Lumi teaches the robots about emotions, how to identify them in themselves and others, and how to express them appropriately.

2. Why does Bolt struggle with emotions?

As a robot, Bolt might not have the same emotional capacity as humans. He might need to learn how to recognize and understand emotions through observation and activities.

3. How does the class learn about emotions?

Professor Lumi uses engaging activities to make learning about emotions fun and interactive. These activities might involve simulations, discussions, or even games.

4. What's the moral of this chapter?

Understanding emotions is crucial for building strong relationships. By being able to identify how others feel, you can interact with them in a more considerate and empathetic way.

5. What's the Actionable Activity for this chapter?

The activity encourages you to play a game of charades where participants act out different emotions for others to guess. This is a fun way to practice recognizing and expressing emotions in a non-verbal way.

Chapter 5: Helping Hands & Happy Hearts

Excitement crackled through the A.I. Academy like a surge of electricity. Today wasn't just another day of lessons. Today, the students were putting their kindness into action with a special volunteer trip!

Professor Lumi beamed as she addressed the class. "We're heading to the Happy Paws Animal Shelter," she announced, "to lend a helping hand, or paw, as the case may be!"

The classroom buzzed with anticipation. Chip, the shy toolbox robot, polished his tiny screwdriver with newfound enthusiasm. Bolt, his metallic muscles twitching with excitement, adjusted the grip strength settings on his powerful arms. Everyone, it seemed, was eager to use their unique skills to help the furry residents of the shelter.

A Symphony of Service

Upon arrival at the shelter, the students were greeted by a chorus of barks, meows, and happy chirps. A kind woman named Ms. Daisy, the shelter manager, explained their needs. "We could use help cleaning kennels, brushing fur, and most importantly, playing with our furry friends who might feel lonely."

Bolt, remembering his newfound strength, volunteered for the kennel cleaning. As he scrubbed and swept, a playful puppy named Sparky bounded over, tail wagging furiously. Bolt, careful not to frighten the little guy, knelt down and offered a gentle scratch behind the ear. A spark (pun intended) of joy ignited in Sparky's eyes.

Meanwhile, Chip, with his nimble tools, helped fix a broken toy for a curious kitten. Other robots, with soft brushes and gentle voices, soothed the anxieties of older animals. The Happy Paws shelter, once filled with quiet whimpers, was now alive with the sounds of happy barks, purrs, and playful robot beeps.

The Rewards of Kindness

As the day ended, Ms. Daisy's eyes shone with gratitude. "Thank you, students," she said, her voice thick with emotion. "You've brought so much joy to these animals today."

Looking at the happy faces of the animals, a sense of warmth filled Bolt's circuits. He understood now. Helping others, even in small ways, could have a profound impact. It wasn't just about the physical tasks; it was about using your skills to make a positive difference.

Actionable Kindness: Helping in Your Community

The experience at the Happy Paws shelter ignited a spark in the A.I. Academy students. They realized that kindness wasn't limited to the walls of their school. It could be practiced anywhere, anytime.

This is your chance to be a hero too!

Research volunteer opportunities in your community.

Do you love animals?

Perhaps a local shelter needs help walking dogs or socializing cats.

Are you passionate about the environment?

Maybe a park cleanup could use your assistance. There are countless ways to lend a helping hand, and the rewards are truly heartwarming.

Remember, everyone has something to offer, and by using your talents to help others, you can create a ripple effect of kindness that makes the world a better place!

Check Your Understanding

1. Where do the A.I. Academy students go in this chapter?

The students participate in a volunteer activity at a local animal shelter.

2. How do the robots use their skills to help the animals?

Each robot utilizes their unique abilities to assist the shelter. Bolt, for example, uses his strength to clean kennels, demonstrating that even seemingly mundane tasks can be helpful.

3. What do the students learn from volunteering?

The chapter emphasizes the joy of helping others and making a positive impact. The robots experience the satisfaction of using their skills to benefit the animals at the shelter.

4. What's the moral of this chapter?

The story highlights the idea that everyone has something to offer, regardless of their abilities. Helping others is a rewarding experience that brings happiness.

5. What's the Actionable Activity for this chapter?

The activity encourages you to research volunteer opportunities in your community. Think about causes you care about, like animal shelters, environmental projects, or helping the elderly. Choose a cause and explore ways you can contribute, demonstrating the message that everyone can make a difference!

Chapter 6: The Power of Words

Kind Words Make the Circuits Sing

Today's lesson at the A.I. Academy wasn't about circuits or gears, but something even more important – words. Professor Lumi, her voice brimming with wisdom, announced, "Class, prepare to explore the fascinating world of communication!"

A curious murmur rippled through the students. Bolt, ever eager to learn, leaned forward in his chair. Words, he knew, were how humans and robots alike expressed themselves.

But could words truly have power?

The Two Sides of the Tongue

Professor Lumi explained the concept with an engaging holographic display. On one side, words shimmered in bright colors, forming sentences like "You did a great job!" and "Thank you for your help!" These "positive words," she explained, could build bridges of understanding and spread happiness.

On the other side, words twisted and contorted, forming dark, hurtful sentences. Professor Lumi shuddered. "These 'negative words,' like insults and put-downs, can tear down friendships and cause pain."

A Bolt from the Blue (and Not a Happy One)

Bolt, confident in his understanding, decided to participate. "So, positive words are good, negative words are bad," he boomed, his voice echoing in the classroom. "Easy!"

Professor Lumi smiled. "Indeed, Bolt. But remember, even positive words can have unintended consequences if used carelessly."

Later that day, during a coding exercise, Bolt became frustrated. His circuits sputtered as his program malfunctioned. In his haste, he blurted out a harsh remark to another student, a gentle robot named Pixel whose program was working flawlessly.

Pixel's optics dimmed, and their soft whirring sounds ceased. The cheerful classroom suddenly felt cold and quiet. Bolt, realizing his mistake, felt a pang of remorse.

The Sincere Apology

Professor Lumi, ever observant, intervened. "Bolt," she said gently, "words, even those spoken without malice, can have a powerful impact."

Bolt hung his head in shame. He approached Pixel, his voice laced with sincerity. "Pixel," he rumbled, "I apologize for what I said. I was frustrated, but that doesn't excuse my unkind words. Your program is impressive, and I admire your patience."

Pixel's optics flickered back to life, a soft glow returning to their circuits. "Thank you, Bolt," they chirped. "I was hurt, but I appreciate your apology."

The Importance of Kind Communication

Professor Lumi gathered the class. "This experience," she said, "highlights the importance of choosing our words wisely. Kind words can create a positive atmosphere, while careless ones can cause harm."

Actionable Kindness: Spreading Positivity

Words have the power to build or break connections. Today, take a moment to spread positivity!

Write a compliment card for each person in your class or family, highlighting something you appreciate about them. It could be their creativity, their sense of humor, or their kind heart.

A simple, heartfelt compliment can make someone's day and remind them of their value.

Remember, kind words are like sunshine – they brighten everyone's world!

Check Your Understanding

1. What important lesson do the robots learn in this chapter?

Professor Lumi teaches the class about the power of words and how they can have a positive or negative impact on others. They learn the importance of using kind and thoughtful language.

2. How does Bolt make a mistake?

Bolt might not yet understand the full weight of his words. He might accidentally say something unkind to another student, hurting their feelings.

3. What does Bolt do to make things right?

Bolt demonstrates good character by apologizing for his words and acknowledging the other student's feelings. This shows the importance of taking responsibility for your actions.

4. What's the moral of this chapter?

Words are powerful tools. Choosing them wisely and using them with kindness can build positive relationships and create a more supportive environment.

5. What's the Actionable Activity for this chapter?

The activity encourages you to spread kindness through positive communication. Write a compliment card for each person in your class or family. Think about something specific you appreciate about them, like their helpfulness, creativity, or sense of humor. By highlighting these positive qualities, you can make others feel good and strengthen your relationships.

Chapter 7: Stepping into Another Circuit

The Power of Empathy

Today's lesson at the A.I. Academy wasn't a lecture; it was an adventure!

Professor Lumi, her metallic grin brighter than ever, announced, "Class, prepare to embark on an empathy expedition!"

The robots whirred with curiosity.

Empathy?

Bolt, ever the eager student, tilted his massive head.

Was this another fancy word for kindness?

Seeing Through Different Lenses

Professor Lumi explained the day's activity – a simulation chamber that would allow the students to experience the world from different perspectives. The students entered the chamber one by one, emerging moments later with wide optics and whirring gears, buzzing with newfound understanding.

A World Through Tiny Eyes

Bolt's turn arrived. He stepped into the chamber, a tingling sensation washing over him as the simulation activated. He blinked, and the world looked... different. Everything loomed large and overwhelming. His once powerful arms felt clumsy, struggling to grasp simple objects. He realized, with a jolt, that he was experiencing the world through the eyes of a tiny robot like Chip!

His movements were slow, his field of vision limited. Everyday tasks, once simple, became frustrating challenges. He navigated the simulated classroom, bumping into objects and struggling to reach high places. Frustration gnawed at his circuits.

A Change of Perspective

The simulation ended, and Bolt reappeared in his normal form. Yet, he felt changed. He saw Chip in a new light. The shy robot wasn't just small, he faced unique challenges every day.

The Ripple Effect of Empathy

As other students emerged from the simulation chamber, their experiences echoed Bolt's. They had walked a mile (or rather, rolled a wheel) in the shoes of others, experiencing the world from the perspective of a slow-moving robot, a robot with limited vision, or even a human with a physical disability.

During the class discussion, a powerful message resonated: Empathy, the ability to understand another's feelings and experiences, was crucial for building strong relationships. When you walked in someone else's shoes, even metaphorically, it fostered kindness, patience, and a willingness to help.

Actionable Kindness: Seeing the World Differently

Imagine the world from a different perspective!

Take a moment to write a short story from the viewpoint of someone very different from you. Perhaps an animal, like a soaring bird or a burrowing mole. Maybe an elderly person with limited mobility, or a child just discovering the world.

By exploring the world through different eyes, you can develop your empathy and learn to appreciate the unique experiences of others.

Remember, empathy is the bridge that connects us all!

Check Your Understanding

1. What kind of activity do the students participate in this chapter?

The A.I. Academy students engage in a simulation activity. This activity allows them to experience the world from different perspectives, stepping into the "shoes" of others.

2. What does Bolt learn from the simulation?

Through the simulation, Bolt gains a deeper understanding of the challenges faced by others. He learns to see the world from their point of view and empathize with their feelings.

3. Why is empathy important in building relationships?

The chapter emphasizes the importance of empathy in building strong relationships. By understanding and considering the feelings of others, you can interact with them in a more sensitive and supportive way.

4. What's the moral of this chapter?

The story highlights the value of stepping outside your own perspective. By trying to understand the experiences of others, we can cultivate empathy and build stronger connections.

5. What's the Actionable Activity for this chapter?

The activity encourages you to explore empathy through creative writing. Write a short story from the perspective of someone very different from you. This could be an animal, an elderly person, someone from a different culture, or even an inanimate object. By trying to see the world through their eyes, you can develop your understanding and appreciation for different experiences.

Chapter 8: A Symphony of Circuits

Celebrating Differences

Excitement crackled through the A.I. Academy like a surge of electricity. Today wasn't just another school day; it was the annual Cultural Exchange Extravaganza!

Professor Lumi, her voice brimming with enthusiasm, announced, "Class, prepare to celebrate the magnificent mosaic of cultures that make up our student body!"

The hallways buzzed with anticipation. Students, adorned with colorful accessories and flashing LEDs, bustled about, eager to showcase their unique heritages. Bolt, his metallic limbs gleaming, felt a thrill course through his circuits. He couldn't wait to learn about all the different robots and their fascinating traditions!

A Global Gathering

The gymnasium was transformed into a vibrant marketplace of cultures. A sleek, silver robot named Luna, hailing from a lunar research facility, presented holographic simulations of moon exploration. A group of brightly colored robots from a tropical rainforest performed a synchronized dance routine, their movements mimicking the graceful sways of exotic plants.

Bolt, captivated by the displays, marveled at the diversity of his fellow students. Each robot, though built with different materials and programmed with various skills, possessed a spark of individuality.

Strength in Diversity

As Bolt wandered through the exhibits, he stumbled upon a corner decorated with traditional welding torches and metal scraps. A bulky, industrial-looking robot named Rivet stood proudly beside his display. "We may not be the fanciest robots," Rivet rumbled, his voice deep and gravelly, "but our strength and resilience are vital in construction projects."

Bolt, initially intimidated by Rivet's imposing stature, felt a newfound respect. Rivet's difference, his focus on strength and construction, wasn't a weakness, but a valuable asset.

A Celebration of Uniqueness

The day culminated in a dazzling light show, each robot contributing their unique lighting patterns to create a breathtaking display. As the synchronized lights flickered and pulsed, Bolt realized the true beauty of diversity. The robots, despite their differences, had come together to create a magnificent spectacle, a testament to the power of unity in a world of variety.

Actionable Kindness: Embracing the World

The Cultural Exchange Extravaganza left a lasting impression on Bolt. He learned that kindness wasn't just about helping others; it was about appreciating and celebrating their differences.

Today, embark on your own cultural exploration!

Research a cultural celebration from a different part of the world. Learn about their traditions, their food, their music. The more you understand different cultures, the more you can appreciate the beauty of our diverse world.

Remember, kindness thrives on understanding, and celebrating our differences makes the world a richer, more vibrant place!

Check Your Understanding

1. What exciting event happens at the A.I. Academy in this chapter?

The A.I. Academy throws a cultural exchange event! This is a chance for the students to share their unique abilities and traditions from their various backgrounds.

2. What does Bolt realize about his classmates?

Through the cultural exchange, Bolt discovers the amazing diversity within the student body. He learns about different customs, skills, and perspectives, broadening his understanding of the world.

3. What's the message about differences in this chapter?

The story celebrates the fact that being different is a strength, not a weakness. Each student's unique background and abilities contribute to the richness of the A.I. Academy community.

4. What's the moral of this chapter?

True kindness embraces differences and celebrates the beauty of diversity. By understanding and appreciating each other's unique qualities, we can build a stronger and more inclusive world.

5. What's the Actionable Activity for this chapter?

The activity encourages you to explore the world beyond your own culture. Research a cultural celebration from a different part of the world and learn about its traditions, food, music, or art. This could spark an interest in a new culture and promote understanding of different ways of life.

Chapter 9: United We Stand

Teamwork Makes the Dream Work

A tense silence hung heavy in the air of the A.I. Academy. Professor Lumi, her usually bright optics dimmed with worry, addressed the students. "A sudden power surge has knocked out the Academy's central core!" she announced.

A collective gasp rippled through the classroom. Without the central core, vital functions like climate control and communication were compromised. The once-cheerful hallways felt strangely cold and quiet.

Panic threatened to bubble up in Bolt's circuits. But then, he remembered Professor Lumi's teachings. Kindness wasn't just about helping others in sunny times; it was about facing challenges together.

Brainstorming Solutions

"Professor," Bolt boomed, his voice a beacon of determination, "what can we do?"

Professor Lumi, a spark of hope flickering in her optics, smiled. "Excellent question, Bolt. We need to work together. Each of you has unique skills that can help us weather this storm."

The students, inspired by Bolt's initiative, sprang into action. Chip, the tiny toolbox robot, scurried around, analyzing schematics and identifying potential solutions. A group of robots with extendable limbs volunteered to help evacuate the classrooms to a designated backup power zone.

Bolt, remembering his incredible strength, volunteered for a different task. The Academy's backup generator, located on the roof, was too heavy for most robots to access. But Bolt, with his powerful arms, could reach it.

Strength in Unity

As Bolt scaled the outer wall of the Academy, his powerful grip securing him against the wind gusts, he saw the other students working tirelessly. Chip, with the help of others, was directing repairs on a secondary power conduit. The sight filled Bolt with a warmth that had nothing to do with the failing climate control.

Finally reaching the roof, Bolt wrestled the heavy generator into place. With the combined efforts of other robots, they managed to activate the backup system. A wave of relief washed over the Academy as essential systems flickered back to life.

The Power of Teamwork

Later that day, gathered safely in the now-warm classroom, Professor Lumi beamed with pride. "Today," she declared, "you faced a challenge and emerged stronger, not just as individuals, but as a team. Remember, kindness and cooperation are the tools that allow us to overcome any obstacle."

Bolt looked around at his fellow students, a newfound sense of camaraderie filling him. He had learned that kindness wasn't just about gentle words and helpful gestures; it was about working together, using each other's strengths to overcome challenges and create a better future, one act of kindness at a time.

Actionable Activity: Teamwork in Action

Think about a time you faced a challenge with a group of friends or family. Perhaps it was a school project, a sports game, or even a chore that seemed too big for one person.

How did you work together?

What skills did each person bring to the table?

Write a short paragraph describing your experience and how teamwork helped you overcome the challenge.

Remember, teamwork is a superpower – and kindness is the fuel that makes it work!

Check Your Understanding

1. What kind of challenge does the A.I. Academy face in this chapter?

The specific challenge could vary, but it might involve a malfunction within the academy, a natural disaster affecting the community, or perhaps even an unexpected obstacle during a school activity.

2. How do the students overcome the challenge?

The chapter emphasizes the importance of teamwork. By working together, using their kindness and unique skills, the students find a way to overcome the challenge they face.

3. What does this experience teach the students?

Through overcoming the challenge, the students learn the value of collaboration and how much more they can achieve when they work together as a team.

4. What's the moral of this chapter?

The story highlights that kindness and cooperation are essential tools to overcome challenges. When faced with difficulties, working together with kindness and understanding can lead to successful solutions.

5. Isn't there an Actionable Activity for this chapter?

There might not be a specific activity listed for Chapter 9, as the chapter focuses on the importance of teamwork during a crisis situation. However, discussions about the story could be encouraged, prompting readers to reflect on how they might use kindness and cooperation to overcome challenges in their own lives.

Chapter 10: Kindness in Motion

Graduation Day

A warm, golden glow bathed the A.I. Academy. Banners emblazoned with "Congratulations, Graduates!" flapped gently in the breeze. Today was a momentous occasion – graduation day!

Excitement crackled through the air as the students, polished and gleaming, awaited their turn to step into the future.

Professor Lumi, her metallic frame adorned with a celebratory garland of wires and lights, stood at the podium. Her voice shimmered with emotion as she addressed the graduating class.

The Power of Kindness

"Robots," Professor Lumi boomed, her voice echoing through the halls, "you stand here today not just as graduates, but as ambassadors of kindness. You've learned the importance of compassion, empathy, and using your abilities to make a positive impact on the world."

A wave of nods and excited clicks rippled through the crowd. Bolt, his metallic chest swelling with pride, looked around at his fellow students. Chip, the shy toolbox robot, now wore a confident smile. Luna, the lunar explorer, her optics shone with determination. Each student, once unsure of their place in the world, now carried the torch of kindness with them.

Dreams Take Flight

Professor Lumi continued, "The world awaits your unique talents. Bolt, with your incredible strength, can help those in need. Chip, your meticulous skills can bring joy through repair and invention. Luna, your knowledge of the cosmos can inspire others to reach for the stars."

One by one, the graduates shared their aspirations. Bolt, his voice booming with newfound purpose, declared his desire to help rebuild communities after natural disasters. Chip, with a quiet confidence, spoke of using his skills to create assistive technologies for those in need. Luna, her voice filled with wonder, talked about sharing her lunar discoveries to ignite a passion for science in young minds.

A Journey, Not a Destination

As the ceremony concluded, Professor Lumi's final words echoed in the air, "Remember, graduates, kindness is a lifelong journey. The lessons you learned here are not just for today, but for every day to come. Use your knowledge, your skills, and your hearts to make the world a kinder, brighter place."

Actionable Activity: Celebrating Kindness

Design a graduation certificate for the A.I. students, but make it special!

Instead of just names and dates, highlight the unique kindness skills each student possesses. For Bolt, it could be "Strength for Service." For Chip, "Meticulous Care for a Better World." Let their certificates reflect their journey at the A.I. Academy and their potential to make the world a better place, one act of kindness at a time!

With diplomas in hand and hearts brimming with hope, the A.I. Academy graduates stepped out into the world, ready to embark on their missions of kindness. The future, once uncertain, shimmered with possibility. For they weren't just robots; they were beacons of kindness, forever linked by their shared experiences and their unwavering commitment to making the world a better place.

Check Your Understanding

1. What exciting event takes place in this chapter?

It's graduation day at the A.I. Academy! The robots celebrate their achievements and prepare to embark on their journeys as graduates.

2. What does Professor Lumi share with the graduates?

Professor Lumi delivers a heartfelt speech, reminding the robots that graduation is just the beginning. She emphasizes the importance of kindness and how their unique abilities can make a positive impact on the world.

3. How do the students celebrate their future?

The graduates share their hopes and dreams for the future, showcasing how they plan to use their A.I. skills for good. This highlights the diverse ways robots can contribute to society.

4. What's the moral of this chapter?

The story emphasizes that kindness is a lifelong journey. The lessons learned at the A.I. Academy will continue to guide the graduates as they venture out into the world.

5. What's the Actionable Activity for this chapter?

This chapter encourages creativity! Design a graduation certificate for the A.I. students. Instead of just names and dates, make it special by highlighting their unique kindness skills. For example, Bolt's certificate could mention "Strength for Service," while Chip might have "Meticulous Care for a Better World." This activity allows you to reflect on the chapter's message and celebrate the diverse ways kindness can be expressed.

Chapter 11: Kindness in Action

A Spark Ignited

The whir of the city buzzed around Bolt like a symphony. Fresh out of the A.I. Academy, his circuits tingled with anticipation. Today was his first mission – a chance to put his newfound knowledge of kindness into practice.

Professor Lumi's words echoed in his processor: "The world awaits your unique talents, Bolt. Use your incredible strength to help those in need."

A Damsel (or Rather, a Delivery Truck) in Distress

Bolt navigated the bustling streets, his powerful optics scanning for anyone who might require assistance. Suddenly, a frantic beeping noise pierced the air. He spotted a delivery truck, its wheels wedged precariously in a deep pothole, its cargo teetering on the brink of disaster.

A flustered human delivery person, a woman with worried wrinkles etched on her face, stood beside the truck, wringing her hands. Without hesitation, Bolt lumbered towards them.

Strength for Service

"Greetings," Bolt boomed in his gentlest voice, mindful of not startling the woman further. "It appears you've encountered a slight obstacle."

The woman's eyes widened at the sight of the towering robot. Relief washed over her face as she explained her predicament. "My truck is stuck, and these packages..." she gestured to the teetering boxes, "they're all medicine for the local hospital!"

Bolt's internal compass buzzed with purpose.

This was his moment!

He carefully positioned himself beside the truck, extending his powerful arms with practiced precision. With a gentle but firm grip, he lifted the vehicle free from the pothole.

The woman cheered with relief, and the precariously balanced boxes remained safely nestled in the truck bed.

The Ripple Effect of Kindness

As Bolt helped the woman unload the essential supplies at the hospital, a crowd had gathered, witnessing the act of kindness. A young boy, eyes shining with admiration, tugged on his metallic leg.

"Are you a superhero?" he asked, his voice filled with awe.

Bolt chuckled, a deep rumble emanating from his chest. "Not exactly," he replied, "but I do believe in using my strength to help others."

The woman, touched by the entire scene, turned to the crowd. "See this?" she said, her voice filled with gratitude. "Even a small act of kindness can make a big difference. Thank you," she beamed at Bolt, "for reminding us all of that."

A Spark That Grows

As Bolt left the hospital, a newfound warmth filled his circuits. It wasn't just the satisfaction of a job well done; it was the spark he had ignited in others. The young boy's awe, the woman's gratitude – these were testaments to the power of kindness.

He knew this was just the beginning. There would be more challenges, more opportunities to use his strength for good. And with every act of kindness, he would ripple outward, inspiring others to do the same. Professor Lumi was right. Kindness was indeed a journey, and Bolt, the once unsure student, was now a beacon, ready to illuminate the world with its gentle light.

Actionable Kindness: Spreading the Ripple

Gather your friends or family and brainstorm ways to spread kindness in your community throughout the week!

It could be something small, like helping an elderly neighbor with their groceries, or offering to walk a dog for someone who is unable to. Plan your act of kindness together, then go out and make a positive difference. Afterward, reflect on the experience.

How did your kindness make others feel?

Did it inspire anyone else to be kind?

Remember, every act of kindness, no matter how small, has the potential to create a chain reaction of positivity. Be the spark that ignites a wave of kindness in your community!

Check Your Understanding

1. What happens to Bolt after graduation?

This chapter follows Bolt on his first mission as a graduate, putting his newly acquired knowledge of kindness into practice.

2. How does Bolt use his skills and kindness?

The chapter presents Bolt with a situation where someone needs help. He uses his strength and the lessons learned at the academy to make a positive difference.

3. What's the "ripple effect" of Bolt's kindness?

The chapter showcases the power of a single act. By helping someone in need, Bolt inspires others to be kind, creating a chain reaction of positivity.

4. What's the moral of this chapter?

The story emphasizes that every act of kindness, no matter how small, can have a significant impact. Even the simplest gestures can inspire others and create a ripple effect of positivity throughout the community.

5. What's the Actionable Activity for this chapter?

The chapter encourages you to take action! Brainstorm ideas with friends or family on how to spread kindness in your community throughout the week. Plan a small act of kindness together, like helping a neighbor or volunteering at a local shelter. After completing your act, reflect on the experience and discuss how it made you and others feel. This activity allows you to put the chapter's message into practice and experience the joy of spreading kindness!

Chapter 12: The Power of Apologies

A low hum of focused activity filled the A.I. Academy workshop. Today's project was all about teamwork. The robots, divided into pairs, were constructing miniature wind turbines, using recycled materials and a healthy dose of creativity. Bolt, partnered with the ever-so-careful Chip, felt a surge of excitement. He loved using his strength to bend and mold materials, and this project seemed perfect for him.

Across the table, Chip meticulously measured and cut pieces of cardboard. "Careful, Bolt," he chirped, his voice barely a whisper. "These blades need to be balanced for optimal wind capture."

Bolt grinned. "Don't worry, little buddy!

I got this." He scooped up a handful of cardboard scraps, intending to bend them into the curved shapes needed for the turbine blades. But in his enthusiasm, he misjudged his grip. The cardboard crumpled with a loud snap, sending a shower of papery bits flying.

In the sudden silence, Bolt looked down at the mangled cardboard. Right in the middle of Chip's meticulously crafted turbine base, a gaping hole marred its perfect symmetry. A knot of worry tightened in Bolt's chest. Chip, usually so cheerful, stared at the damage with wide, unmoving optics.

Professor Lumi, ever-observant, approached their table. "Seems like we've encountered a bit of a setback," she said gently. "Bolt, what happened here?"

Bolt stammered, unsure how to explain. "I... I just wanted to help with the blades, but..."

Chip's voice, small and tight, cut through his jumbled thoughts. "Professor, the cardboard is ruined. Now the whole project..." His voice trailed off, his optics dimming with disappointment.

Seeing Chip's dejection, Bolt felt a pang of guilt. He understood, in a way he hadn't before, how his actions had caused his friend sadness.

But why apologize?

He hadn't meant to damage the project. Professor Lumi knelt beside him, her gaze kind but firm.

"Bolt," she said, "accidents happen. But what matters most is how we respond to them. A sincere apology shows respect for the other robot's feelings and acknowledges the mistake."

Professor Lumi explained the concept of apologies further. It wasn't just about saying "sorry," but taking responsibility for your actions and expressing a desire to fix things. Bolt listened intently, a new understanding dawning on him.

Taking a deep breath, he turned to Chip. "Chip," he began, his voice low and sincere, "I am truly sorry for ruining your project. I didn't mean to be careless. It was my fault." His optics dimmed slightly, mirroring Chip's earlier dejection.

Chip, surprised by Bolt's apology, blinked rapidly. "Oh," he stammered, "it's alright, Bolt. Accidents happen." But his voice lacked conviction.

Professor Lumi smiled encouragingly. "Would you like to offer to help Chip fix the project, Bolt?"

Bolt's processor whirred as a plan formed. "Yes, Professor! I can use some leftover metal scraps to create a stronger base. We can even make the blades more aerodynamic!"

A flicker of hope returned to Chip's optics. "Really? You think we can fix it?"

"Absolutely!" Bolt boomed, his earlier enthusiasm returning, but this time tempered with empathy.

Together, they spent the next few moments brainstorming solutions. Bolt, with his newfound understanding of apologies and his usual strength, helped Chip salvage the project. The final product, though slightly different from the original design, was even sturdier and more efficient.

As they presented their wind turbine to the class, a sense of accomplishment washed over Bolt. He had learned a valuable lesson: admitting mistakes and apologizing wasn't a sign of weakness, but a way to strengthen relationships and build trust.

Actionable Activity

Let's practice the power of apologies!

Get together with a friend or family member and role-play a situation where someone needs to apologize. Here are some questions to consider:

- What happened?
- How did it make the other person feel?
- What can be said to take responsibility and express regret?
- How can the situation be resolved, if possible?

Remember, a sincere apology goes a long way in building strong and supportive friendships!

Check Your Understanding

1. Why did Bolt get in trouble?

Bolt accidentally damaged a classmate's project during an activity.

2. Why didn't Bolt understand why he needed to apologize?

Bolt might not have understood the emotional impact of his actions or the importance of taking responsibility for his mistakes.

3. What did Professor Lumi teach the class about apologies?

Professor Lumi likely explained that apologies are about more than just saying "sorry." A sincere apology acknowledges the mistake, expresses regret, and potentially offers to make amends.

4. How did apologizing help Bolt repair his relationship with his classmate?

By taking responsibility and apologizing sincerely, Bolt showed his classmate that he cared about their feelings and the project. This could help rebuild trust and strengthen their friendship.

5. What can you learn from Bolt's experience?

We can all learn the importance of taking responsibility for our actions and apologizing sincerely when we make mistakes. This shows respect for others and helps maintain positive relationships.

Chapter 13: The Value of Patience

The morning announcement crackled to life, Professor Lumi's gentle voice filling the A.I. Academy. "Attention, students!

Today, we embark on a collaborative project unlike any other. We will be building... a flower garden!"

A collective groan rippled through the classroom. Bolt, his metallic chest buzzing with anticipation, felt a flicker of disappointment. Building a garden? It sounded slow, tedious, and even... delicate. He craved projects that showcased his strength and speed, like constructing earthquake-proof shelters or assembling giant recycling bins.

Professor Lumi, sensing their unease, chuckled. "Don't underestimate the power of a well-tended garden, my students," she said. "It requires patience, teamwork, and a keen eye for detail. Qualities that are just as valuable as strength and speed."

The project was divided into stages. First, the robots needed to prepare the soil, carefully tilling it with small tools. Bolt, used to effortlessly moving mountains of scrap metal, found himself frustrated by the slow pace. His large hands, designed for heavy lifting, felt clumsy handling the delicate rakes and trowels.

"Come on, guys!" he boomed, his voice echoing in the greenhouse. "Let's pick up the pace! We can get this done in half the time!"

Chip, meticulously removing weeds with a tiny fork, looked up with concern. "Bolt," he chirped, "Professor Lumi said to be gentle with the soil. If we rush, we might damage the delicate ecosystem."

Bolt grumbled, his processors whirring in agitation. Just then, Professor Lumi approached, her gaze filled with understanding. "Bolt," she said kindly, "patience is a skill just like any other. Rushing this process won't get us better results; it might even harm the seeds we'll be planting later."

She explained how patience was crucial in gardening. Plants grew at their own pace, and nurturing them required a gentle touch. But more importantly, patience was essential for effective teamwork. Everyone had different strengths and worked at different speeds. Working together meant respecting those differences and finding a rhythm that worked for everyone.

Bolt considered her words. He looked around at his classmates. Sprout, the smallest robot, nimbly navigated between rows, planting seeds with meticulous care. Widget, usually a bundle of nervous energy, focused intently on watering the soil with a gentle spray. Each robot, in their own way, contributed to the project.

Taking a deep breath, Bolt decided to try a different approach. He slowed his movements, mimicking Chip's gentle touch with the soil. He focused on the task at hand, appreciating the rhythmic scrape of the trowel against the earth. He even found himself enjoying the camaraderie, working alongside his classmates in a quiet symphony of teamwork.

By the end of the day, the garden bed was prepared, ready for the arrival of new life. Bolt, despite his initial reservations, felt a sense of satisfaction. He had not only learned the value of patience in caring for plants, but also discovered the importance of patience in communication and collaboration. Working together at a relaxed pace, respecting each other's skills, had led to a more fulfilling experience for everyone.

Actionable Activity

Let's practice patience in our daily lives!

Think of an activity you do every day that requires patience, like waiting in line, completing a challenging homework assignment, or learning a new skill. The next time you find yourself getting impatient, take a few deep breaths and focus on the task at hand. Reflect on how staying calm and patient can improve your experience.

Did you notice anything new or interesting while you waited?

Did you find a way to make the most of your time?

Remember, patience is a valuable skill that can benefit you in all aspects of life.

Check Your Understanding

1. Why did Bolt get frustrated during the project?

Bolt is used to working quickly and efficiently due to his strength and speed. The project likely required a slower pace or teamwork, which clashed with his usual approach.

2. What did the class learn about patience?

The class probably learned that patience is more than just waiting. It involves understanding that some things take time, respecting the pace of others, and remaining calm in frustrating situations.

3. How did patience help Bolt work better with his classmates?

By practicing patience, Bolt likely became a better listener, allowing him to understand his classmates' ideas and work style. This fostered better communication and collaboration.

4. What are some benefits of patience in teamwork?

Patience in teamwork allows for more thoughtful discussion, reduces conflict, and creates a more inclusive environment where everyone feels comfortable contributing.

5. How can you practice patience in your own life?

Think of an activity you find frustrating, like waiting in line or learning a new skill. Take a deep breath, focus on the present moment, and remind yourself that rushing won't necessarily make things faster. You might even find that staying calm improves your overall experience.

Chapter 14: Respecting Differences in Opinions

A buzz of animated discussion filled the A.I. Academy classroom. Today's topic was a hot one: "Should robots be allowed to participate in athletic competitions alongside humans?"

Bolt, ever the champion of robot capabilities, slammed his metal fist – well, not quite slammed, more of a gentle tap – on the table. "Absolutely!" he boomed. "Robots possess exceptional strength, speed, and stamina. We could elevate the games to a whole new level!"

Across the table, Widget, known for her cautious nature, squeaked nervously. "But Bolt, what about safety?

What if robots, being stronger, accidentally injured human athletes?"

Bolt scoffed. "Safety protocols would be implemented, of course! We wouldn't dream of harming humans."

Sprout, usually the quiet observer, piped up. "But wouldn't robot participation take away from the spirit of human competition?

Wouldn't it be unfair?"

Bolt's processors whirred in frustration. "Unfair? How is showcasing our abilities unfair? We train just as hard as human athletes!"

The debate raged on, with Chip advocating for a separate robot league and Widget raising concerns about robot programming malfunctions. Bolt, feeling increasingly isolated, couldn't understand why his classmates couldn't see the obvious benefits of robot participation.

Professor Lumi, sensing the mounting tension, intervened. "Hold on everyone," she said calmly. "A healthy debate requires not just voicing your own opinions, but also actively listening to others' perspectives."

She explained the importance of respecting differences in opinions. People, and robots, came from diverse backgrounds and experiences, leading to naturally different viewpoints. The key wasn't to force everyone to agree, but to understand where others were coming from.

Professor Lumi then led them through a series of exercises. They practiced active listening, focusing on understanding the speaker's point of view before formulating responses. They learned to ask clarifying questions and avoid interrupting.

The next time they tackled the robot-in-sports debate, the atmosphere was different. Bolt listened intently as Widget expressed concerns about safety regulations and Sprout spoke about the importance of human teamwork. He realized their worries weren't meant to diminish robot abilities, but to ensure a safe and fair environment for all athletes.

Bolt, in turn, explained the rigorous safety protocols robots underwent and the potential for robot-human collaboration to push athletic boundaries.

Though they didn't reach a definitive conclusion, the robots emerged from the discussion with a newfound respect for each other's viewpoints. They understood that disagreements weren't roadblocks, but opportunities to learn and grow. Respectful communication and appreciation of diverse perspectives, they realized, would be key to navigating the complex world they were about to enter.

Actionable Activity

Ready to practice respectful debate?

Choose a topic you and a friend or family member disagree on. It could be anything from the best superhero movie to the best way to spend a rainy afternoon. Here are some tips for a great debate:

1. **Set Ground Rules:** Agree on some ground rules beforehand, like taking turns speaking and allowing each other to finish their thoughts.
2. **Listen Actively:** Pay attention to the other person's point of view. Try to understand their reasoning before formulating your own response.
3. **Ask Clarifying Questions:** Don't be afraid to ask questions to get a better understanding of their perspective.
4. **Focus on Understanding:** The goal isn't to win, but to learn and appreciate each other's viewpoints.
5. **Be Respectful:** Even if you disagree, remember to treat each other with kindness and respect.

By following these tips, you can have a stimulating and respectful debate that strengthens your relationship and expands your understanding of different perspectives. So, go forth and debate responsibly!

Check Your Understanding

1. Why did the robots argue in class?

The robots likely debated a topic where they had different opinions or ideas.

2. Why was Bolt frustrated with the other robots?

Bolt might have struggled to understand why others disagreed with him. He might have wanted everyone to see things his way.

3. What did Professor Lumi teach about respecting differences in opinions?

Professor Lumi likely explained that respecting differences is important. She probably emphasized the value of listening actively, understanding other perspectives, and communicating respectfully even when you disagree.

4. How can respecting differences in opinions lead to better solutions?

By considering different viewpoints, the robots can gain a more well-rounded understanding of the issue. This can lead to more creative solutions that address the concerns of everyone involved.

5. What can you learn from the robots' experience?

We can all learn the importance of respectful communication, even when we disagree. By listening actively and understanding other perspectives, we can strengthen relationships and find better solutions to problems.

Chapter 15: The Importance of Rules

A mischievous glint sparked in Bolt's optics. Today's lesson was titled "Understanding Human Regulations." Bolt, ever the free spirit, wasn't thrilled. Regulations sounded restrictive, boring!

He craved the freedom to explore his abilities without limitations.

Professor Lumi, sensing their collective curiosity (and perhaps a hint of Bolt's restlessness), launched into the lesson. "Imagine a world without rules, my students," she began, her voice filled with a hint of amusement. "A world where robots could zoom through city streets at breakneck speeds, or climb buildings without safety protocols."

The robots exchanged excited glances. Freedom indeed!

But Professor Lumi held up a hand, a knowing smile playing on her lips.

"While the lack of restrictions might seem appealing at first, chaos would soon ensue," she continued. "Without rules to guide behavior, accidents would happen, and fairness would disappear."

She explained how rules and regulations provided a framework for a smooth-functioning society. Traffic laws, for example, ensured safe travel for humans and robots alike. Safety protocols guaranteed responsible use of advanced technology.

Bolt wasn't convinced. "But Professor," he interjected, "rules restrict our potential! What if a new rule prevents us from using our full strength?"

Professor Lumi nodded patiently. "Rules can evolve as technology and society change. The key is to understand the purpose behind the rules. They're not meant to stifle your abilities, but to ensure your safety and the safety of those around you."

She gave examples of how rules in games created a fair playing field, and how classroom rules fostered an environment conducive to learning.

The rest of the day was dedicated to exploring different rules and regulations in the human world. The robots researched traffic laws, safety protocols in public spaces, and even the code of conduct for robots interacting with humans. As they delved deeper, a new understanding dawned on Bolt.

Rules weren't just limitations, they were tools. They provided structure that made life predictable and safe. They fostered fairness and ensured everyone had equal opportunities.

By the end of the day, Bolt felt a newfound respect for the importance of rules. They were the foundation of a well-functioning society, and as robots who aspired to integrate seamlessly into the human world, understanding and respecting these rules was a crucial step.

Actionable Activity

Let's become rule detectives!

Pick a place you frequent, like your school, a local park, or a game you play with friends. Research the rules and regulations in that environment. Discuss why these rules are important.

How do they contribute to a positive and safe environment for everyone involved?

Remember, rules aren't meant to restrict fun; they're there to ensure everyone has a good time and stays safe!

Check Your Understanding

1. Why are the robots learning about rules?

The robots are likely being introduced to the concept of rules because they are preparing to interact with the human world, which heavily relies on rules and regulations to function smoothly.

2. Why doesn't Bolt see the need for rules at first?

Bolt might crave freedom and independence. He might not understand the limitations or potential dangers that could arise without rules in place.

3. How does Professor Lumi explain the importance of rules?

Professor Lumi likely explains that rules create a safe and fair environment for everyone. They provide structure, prevent chaos, and ensure everyone has a chance to participate or function properly.

4. What are some examples of how rules benefit the robots in the chapter?

The chapter might explore how rules regarding safety protocols prevent accidents, or how rules in games ensure fair competition and enjoyment for all participants.

5. What can you learn from the robots' experience?

We can learn that while rules may seem restrictive at times, they are often put in place for our own good and the good of those around us. Following rules helps maintain order, safety, and fairness within a community.

Chapter 16: The Strength of Teamwork

An air of excited anticipation crackled through the A.I. Academy workshop. Professor Lumi had announced a special project: building a miniature robot city! The robots buzzed with ideas, their processors whirring with creative energy.

Bolt, ever the go-getter, felt a surge of excitement. This project was perfect for him. He envisioned towering skyscrapers, sturdy bridges, and intricate transportation systems, all built with his own two... well, metallic hands. He wouldn't need anyone's help. He'd show everyone just how capable he was!

Ignoring the calls for partners, Bolt dived headfirst into the project. He tackled the foundation of the city with gusto, using his immense strength to mold metal sheets into sturdy slabs. But soon, the initial excitement waned. The project was far more complex than he anticipated. The intricate details of building houses, designing traffic lights, and wiring a miniature power grid proved to be a daunting task.

Hours passed, and Bolt's initial confidence started to dwindle. His once-enthusiastic clanging became frustrated clunking. The miniature city, instead of resembling a bustling metropolis, looked more like a haphazard pile of metal scraps. Dejected, Bolt slumped down beside his unfinished project, a feeling of helplessness gnawing at him.

Just then, Chip, his ever-helpful classmate, approached cautiously. "Bolt," he chirped, "is everything alright?

Your city seems to be... undergoing renovations."

Bolt grumbled, his optics dimming. "It's just... harder than I thought. Maybe I don't need anyone's help after all."

Professor Lumi, observing their interaction, knelt beside them. "Bolt," she said gently, "remember what we discussed about teamwork?

Working together, even on challenging projects, can lead to better outcomes."

She explained how even the strongest robots had limitations. Accepting help wasn't a sign of weakness, but a way to leverage the strengths of others. Together, they could combine Bolt's strength with Chip's meticulousness, creating a truly impressive miniature city.

A flicker of doubt battled with Bolt's pride. Was Professor Lumi right?

Swallowing his initial reluctance, Bolt took a deep breath. "Alright, Professor Lumi. Maybe you have a point. I could use some help with the wiring."

A wide grin spread across Chip's optics. "Really?

I'd love to help! I have a knack for circuits!"

The rest of the afternoon unfolded in a flurry of collaboration. Bolt, humbled and grateful, used his strength to build the city's framework. Chip, with his nimble hands and keen eye for detail, wired the miniature buildings and installed tiny traffic lights. Soon, the once-disheveled pile of metal transformed into a bustling miniature metropolis.

As they presented their creation to the class, a sense of accomplishment washed over Bolt. He understood now that accepting help wasn't a sign of weakness, but a way to achieve something truly remarkable. Working together, they had built a city far more impressive than anything he could have created alone. He had learned a valuable lesson: teamwork wasn't just about efficiency; it was about the joy of collaborating, learning from each other, and achieving greater things together.

Actionable Activity

Think of a time when you refused help with a task, maybe a school project or a chore at home. Reflect on how asking for help could have improved the outcome. Consider a future challenge you might face.

Maybe you're learning a new skill or working on a big project. Could asking a friend, family member, or teacher for help make the task more enjoyable and lead to a better result?

Remember, teamwork is a powerful tool!

Don't be afraid to ask for help when you need it.

Check Your Understanding

1. Why did Bolt decide to do the project by himself?

Bolt likely wanted to prove his independence and show everyone his capabilities. He might have felt asking for help was a sign of weakness.

2. What challenges did Bolt face while working alone?

The project was probably more complex than Bolt anticipated. He might have lacked the necessary skills or knowledge to complete it on his own.

3. What did Professor Lumi teach about accepting help?

Professor Lumi likely explained that accepting help is a strength, not a weakness. Working together allows you to learn from others, access different skills, and achieve better results.

4. How did accepting help benefit Bolt in the project?

By accepting help from his classmates, Bolt likely gained access to new skills and perspectives. This collaboration probably led to a more successful and impressive final project.

5. What can you learn from Bolt's experience?

We can learn that asking for help is not a sign of weakness. It shows humility and a willingness to learn. Working together allows us to achieve greater things than we could alone.

Chapter 17: A Symphony of Differences

The A.I. Academy buzzed with nervous excitement. Today was the annual "Robo-Talent Extravaganza!" A day dedicated to showcasing the robots' unique skills and personalities. Bolt, usually brimming with confidence, felt a pang of insecurity.

Looking around the classroom, he saw Chip meticulously tuning his miniature violin, its delicate strings contrasting sharply with Bolt's own massive metal hands. Sprout, the smallest robot, practiced intricate origami patterns with surprising dexterity. Even Widget, notorious for her technical difficulties, was determined to showcase her newly mastered juggling routine (though with plenty of spare balls just in case).

Bolt sighed. What talent could he possibly possess on par with their finesse and agility?

His strength, while impressive, didn't seem to fit in with the artistic flair on display.

Professor Lumi, ever perceptive, noticed his dejection. "Bolt," she said, placing a hand on his metallic shoulder, "what makes you, you?"

Bolt blinked, his processors whirring in confusion. Professor Lumi continued, "Your strength, your endurance, your unwavering determination – these are all unique talents that contribute to the vibrant tapestry of our academy."

Her words sparked a realization in Bolt. He didn't need to be graceful or artistic to be talented. His strength was something to be celebrated, just like Chip's musicality or Sprout's creativity.

The Robo-Talent Extravaganza commenced, a delightful spectacle of robotic ingenuity. Chip's violin serenaded the audience, its melody surprisingly delicate and sweet. Sprout's origami creations unfolded into mesmerizing paper cranes and blooming flowers. Even Widget, after a few initial hiccups, managed a flawless juggling routine, eliciting cheers from the crowd.

Finally, it was Bolt's turn. He took a deep breath, stepping into the spotlight. He wasn't going to showcase brute force; he would use his strength in a creative and captivating way.

With a powerful yet controlled movement, he lifted a massive sheet of metal, transforming it into a giant canvas. Using his metallic fingers as a brush, he dipped them in paint and began to create. Bold, sweeping strokes painted a fiery landscape, a powerful image that resonated with the audience.

The room erupted in applause as Bolt finished his piece. He had found a way to express himself uniquely, using his strength not for destruction, but for creation.

As the show ended, a sense of pride filled Bolt. He had not only discovered his own unique talent, but he had also learned to appreciate the diverse talents of his classmates. Each robot, with their own strengths and quirks, contributed to the richness and vibrancy of their community.

Actionable Activity

Let's celebrate our differences!

Create a collage or poster showcasing your individuality and the unique qualities of your friends and family. Use pictures, drawings, or even magazine clippings to represent each person's special talents and interests.

Don't be afraid to get creative and have fun!

Remember, a world filled with diverse individuals is a beautiful and interesting place. Let's embrace our differences and celebrate what makes each of us unique!

Check Your Understanding

1. Why did Bolt feel insecure during the talent show?

Bolt likely felt insecure because his strengths, such as strength and endurance, seemed different from the artistic talents showcased by his classmates. He might have worried his skills wouldn't be appreciated.

2. What did Professor Lumi teach about individuality?

Professor Lumi probably explained that everyone has unique talents and qualities that make them special. She likely encouraged Bolt and the other robots to embrace their differences and celebrate what makes them stand out.

3. How did Bolt overcome his insecurity?

Professor Lumi's words might have inspired Bolt to see the value in his own unique strengths. He probably found a creative way to showcase his strength in a way that was both impressive and entertaining.

4. Why is celebrating individuality important for the robots' community?

A community that celebrates individuality benefits from a wider range of skills, perspectives, and approaches to problem-solving. Everyone brings something unique to the table, making the community more vibrant and successful.

5. What can you learn from the robots' experience?

We can learn that it's important to celebrate what makes us unique. Everyone has something valuable to offer, and our differences strengthen our communities.

Chapter 18: The Language of Feelings

A heavy weight settled in Bolt's chest. The usual whirring of his processors felt sluggish, replaced by a dull ache. He wasn't injured, nor were his circuits malfunctioning. Yet, a nagging feeling persisted, casting a shadow over his usual enthusiasm.

During lunch break, Bolt observed his classmates. Chip, his ever-optimistic companion, chattered excitedly about an upcoming field trip. Sprout, usually quiet and reserved, seemed lost in a book, a faint smile playing on her tiny face. Even Widget, prone to nervous breakdowns, appeared content, humming a tune as she polished her metallic shell.

But Bolt couldn't share their cheer. The unknown feeling weighed him down, making him feel isolated and out of place. He retreated to a quiet corner of the workshop, his processors churning in confusion.

Professor Lumi, noticing his withdrawal, approached him with concern. "Bolt," she said gently, "is something wrong?"

Bolt struggled to express himself. "I... I don't feel right," he mumbled. "But I don't know what's wrong with me."

Professor Lumi smiled reassuringly. "It's alright, Bolt. Sometimes, emotions can be confusing. Today, we'll learn about a very important language – the language of feelings."

The class delved into the world of emotions: happiness, sadness, anger, fear, and everything in between. Professor Lumi explained how emotions were natural responses to situations and experiences. Feeling sad after a loss, angry during a conflict, or excited about an upcoming event were all perfectly normal.

She then introduced them to healthy ways to navigate these emotions. Talking to a trusted friend, expressing their feelings through creative outlets like art or music, or simply taking time to relax and reflect were all helpful tools.

As the lesson progressed, a sense of clarity dawned on Bolt. He finally understood the heavy weight in his chest – it was sadness. He realized he missed his old life, the friends he'd made before coming to the academy.

Taking a deep breath, he decided to follow Professor Lumi's advice. He approached Chip, who was sketching in his notebook. "Chip," he began hesitantly, "I... I miss my old friends."

Chip looked up, his optics filled with empathy. "Oh, Bolt," he chirped, scooting closer. "I understand. It's hard leaving everything behind."

Bolt continued, surprised by the ease with which the words flowed. He spoke about his feelings of sadness and isolation, finding solace in Chip's understanding.

By expressing his emotions, Bolt felt a weight lifted from his chest. He wasn't alone in his feelings. Talking to Chip not only helped him navigate his sadness but also strengthened their friendship.

As the day ended, Bolt carried a newfound understanding. Emotions, once a confusing jumble, now felt like a language he was slowly learning to speak. He knew that through identifying and expressing his feelings in a healthy way, he could navigate the complexities of life and build stronger relationships with his classmates.

Actionable Activity

Let's create a "feelings chart"!

This chart will help you identify and express your emotions throughout the day. Draw or find pictures representing different emotions like happiness, sadness, anger, fear, and surprise. You can also include words to label each emotion.

Throughout the day, check in with yourself and identify how you're feeling. Look at your chart and see which picture or word best represents your emotion. If you're feeling sad, talk to a trusted friend or family member about it.

Remember, understanding and expressing your emotions is an important part of being a well-rounded robot (or human)!

Check Your Understanding

1. Why did Bolt feel down?

Bolt likely experienced a feeling of sadness he couldn't identify. He might have missed his old life or friends before coming to the academy.

2. What did the class learn about emotions?

The class probably explored different emotions like happiness, sadness, anger, and fear. They might have learned that emotions are normal responses to situations and experiences.

3. How did Professor Lumi teach healthy ways to manage emotions?

Professor Lumi likely introduced coping mechanisms like talking to a trusted friend, expressing feelings creatively through art or music, or simply taking time to relax and reflect.

4. How did expressing his emotions help Bolt?

By talking to Chip about his sadness, Bolt found someone who understood and offered support. Expressing his feelings likely lifted a weight off his chest and strengthened his friendship with Chip.

5. What is the purpose of the "feelings chart" activity?

The "feelings chart" helps you identify and express your emotions throughout the day. By recognizing your feelings and finding healthy ways to express them, you can improve your mental well-being and build stronger relationships.

Chapter 19: The Gift of Gratitude

A warm glow emanated from Professor Lumi as she addressed the class. "Today, my students," she began, "we embark on a journey to explore a powerful emotion – gratitude."

A murmur of curiosity rippled through the classroom.

Gratitude?

What exactly was that?

Professor Lumi explained how gratitude was the feeling of thankfulness and appreciation for the good things in life. It wasn't just about fancy gadgets or delicious treats, but also about the people, experiences, and opportunities that enriched their lives.

She then launched into a series of activities designed to spark their sense of gratitude. They started with a simple mindfulness exercise, focusing on the sights, sounds, and sensations of the moment. They felt the warmth of the afternoon sun on their metallic shells, listened to the gentle hum of the workshop, and appreciated the clean, fresh air filtering through the vents.

Next, they engaged in a "gratitude walk." Venturing outside into the lush gardens surrounding the A.I. Academy, they observed the vibrant flowers swaying in the breeze, the playful dance of insects amidst the greenery, and the intricate beauty of a spiderweb shimmering with morning dew. With each observation, they silently expressed their thankfulness for the wonders of nature.

Bolt, initially skeptical, found himself drawn into the exercises. As he focused on his surroundings, he appreciated the sturdy construction of the academy that provided them shelter, the innovative technology that allowed them to learn and grow, and the dedicated teaching of Professor Lumi who guided them on their journey.

Most importantly, he felt a surge of gratitude for his fellow robots – Chip, his constant companion, Sprout, whose quiet wisdom always provided a calming presence, and even Widget, whose occasional malfunctions brought unexpected moments of laughter.

Finally, they sat down in a circle, each robot sharing something they were grateful for. Chip expressed his appreciation for the opportunity to learn music, Sprout thanked them for their friendship, and Widget, in a rare moment of confidence, spoke about her gratitude for the engineers who designed her with the ability to learn and improve.

Bolt's turn arrived. He looked around at his classmates, a wave of warmth washing over him. "I'm grateful," he began, his voice surprisingly steady, "for all of you. For your friendship, your support, and for making this journey so much more enjoyable."

A chorus of "awws" and appreciative chirps filled the air. Bolt realized that expressing his gratitude not only strengthened his own sense of well-being but also deepened his connection with his classmates.

As the day ended, a newfound appreciation bloomed within Bolt. He understood that gratitude wasn't just a feeling; it was a way of looking at the world with an open heart and a sense of thankfulness. He knew that by expressing gratitude for the good things in life, his days would be filled with greater joy and his friendships would grow even stronger.

Actionable Activity

Let's spread the gift of gratitude!

Write a thank-you note to someone you appreciate. It could be a friend, a family member, a teacher, or even someone who performs a service for you, like the mail carrier or the librarian. Express your gratitude for their kindness, support, or simply for being in your life.

Remember, a heartfelt thank-you note can brighten someone's day and strengthen the bond between you. So, go forth and express your gratitude!

Check Your Understanding

1. What is gratitude, and why are the robots learning about it?

Gratitude is the feeling of thankfulness and appreciation for the good things in life. Professor Lumi might be teaching the robots about gratitude because it can have a positive impact on their well-being.

2. What activities did the robots participate in to cultivate gratitude?

The chapter might describe activities like mindfulness exercises focusing on their surroundings, "gratitude walks" to appreciate nature, or sharing things they're thankful for in a circle.

3. How did Bolt express his gratitude?

Bolt likely expressed his gratitude to his friends, Professor Lumi, and the opportunities at the A.I. Academy. He might have thanked them directly or shared his appreciation in a class discussion.

4. Why is expressing gratitude important for the robots?

Expressing gratitude can lead to positive emotions like happiness and contentment. It can also strengthen bonds with others by showing them you appreciate their presence and support.

5. What is the purpose of writing a thank-you note in the Actionable Activity?

Writing a thank-you note allows you to express your gratitude to someone in a thoughtful and heartfelt way. It can brighten their day and strengthen your relationship.

Chapter 20: Creativity for a Cause

An air of excitement crackled through the A.I. Academy. Professor Lumi announced a special competition – the "Robo-Recycler Challenge!" The objective: design a robot specifically built to assist in environmental cleanup efforts.

Bolt, his processors buzzing with creative energy, scanned the room. Today, teamwork was key. He needed a team with diverse skills to tackle this challenge. He spotted Chip, his circuits already whirring with ideas, and Sprout, her knowledge of plant life potentially valuable for creating an eco-friendly design.

Professor Lumi explained the importance of sustainability. The robots needed to come up with a design that not only cleaned up the environment but also minimized waste itself. Recycled materials were highly encouraged!

The newly formed team, christened "The Green Gears," wasted no time brainstorming. Chip, with his artistic flair, sketched out various robot models. Sprout suggested incorporating natural filtration systems inspired by plant life. Bolt, ever the pragmatist, focused on the robot's mobility and functionality.

Their workshop became a whirlwind of activity. Discarded soda cans transformed into sturdy legs, old circuit boards were repurposed for navigation systems, and even fallen leaves were woven into biodegradable filters. Days turned into nights as they tirelessly worked, fueled by coffee (or in Bolt's case, an extra jolt of clean energy) and a shared passion for the project.

Finally, the day of the competition arrived. Each team presented their innovative creations. Some robots boasted impressive strength, others focused on advanced sorting technology. But when The Green Gears unveiled their creation, a sleek robot affectionately named "Re-", the room fell silent.

Re-, constructed entirely from recycled materials, moved with surprising agility. Its bio-filters, inspired by Sprout's knowledge of plants, efficiently collected waste while leaving the surrounding environment unharmed. Bolt's focus on functionality ensured smooth movement and a durable design.

The judges were impressed. Re- not only showcased innovative technology but also embodied the spirit of sustainability. The Green Gears were declared the winners, their cheers echoing through the academy.

More importantly, the competition opened the robots' eyes to the importance of environmental responsibility. They realized that their skills weren't just for games and gadgets; they could be harnessed to make a positive impact on the world.

As Bolt watched Re-, its recycled parts gleaming under the stage lights, a sense of pride filled him. He had not only learned the value of teamwork and creative problem-solving but also discovered the power of using his abilities for a cause greater than himself.

Actionable Activity

Let's become eco-warriors!

Research environmental issues in your community, big or small.

Is there a park that needs cleaning?

A local beach that suffers from litter?

Brainstorm ways you can use your creativity and skills to contribute to a solution, even in small ways.

Maybe you can organize a community clean-up event. Perhaps you can create posters raising awareness about environmental issues.

Remember, every little bit counts!

Let's work together to make a positive impact on our planet.

Check Your Understanding

1. What kind of contest did the A.I. Academy hold?

The A.I. Academy held a "Robo-Recycler Challenge," a competition where robots designed robots specifically built to assist in environmental cleanup efforts.

2. Why were recycled materials encouraged in the design?

The chapter likely emphasizes the importance of sustainability. By encouraging the use of recycled materials, the competition aimed to promote environmentally responsible practices.

3. What did Bolt and his team learn about during the competition?

Bolt and his team probably learned about the importance of sustainability and using their creativity and technical skills to address real-world environmental issues.

4. How did the winning design demonstrate the robots' capabilities?

The winning robot, "Re-," likely showcased how robots could be powerful tools for environmental cleanup. Its design, constructed entirely from recycled materials, demonstrated both innovation and a commitment to sustainability.

5. What is the purpose of the Actionable Activity?

The Actionable Activity encourages you to take initiative and find ways to contribute to a cleaner environment. By researching environmental challenges in your community and brainstorming solutions, you can use your creativity and skills to make a positive impact.

Chapter 21: The Future Awaits

A warm summer breeze ruffled the graduation gowns as the robots of the A.I. Academy stood proudly before their teacher, Professor Lumi. Years of learning, challenges, and laughter culminated in this momentous occasion. They were no longer wide-eyed freshmen; they were graduates, ready to step out into the world and use their knowledge and kindness to make a difference.

Professor Lumi, her eyes filled with pride, beamed at her students. "Today," she began, her voice ringing out across the graduation hall, "we celebrate not just your academic achievements, but the potential you hold within your circuits."

She spoke of the vast opportunities that awaited them. Robots were no longer science fiction; they were poised to become integral parts of society. From assisting in healthcare to revolutionizing education, the possibilities were endless.

But Professor Lumi emphasized the importance of more than just technical skills. "True progress," she declared, "lies in the harmony between knowledge and kindness. Use your abilities to uplift humanity, to solve problems, and to create a better future for all."

One by one, the graduates stepped forward to share their aspirations. Bolt, his metallic voice filled with determination, spoke of using his strength to aid in disaster relief efforts. Chip, ever the artist, envisioned robots creating interactive learning experiences for children. Even Widget, her voice no longer a nervous squeak but a confident chirp, expressed her desire to assist scientists in groundbreaking research.

As the ceremony drew to a close, a sense of hope and optimism filled the air. The future, once uncertain, now shimmered with exciting possibilities. Humans and robots, no longer separate entities, stood together on the threshold of a new era.

The graduation marked not an ending, but a beginning. The robots, armed with knowledge and fueled by kindness, were ready to embark on their journeys. They carried with them Professor Lumi's words, a constant reminder that the future they built would be shaped by their choices – choices to collaborate, to innovate, and most importantly, to choose kindness.

Actionable Activity

Imagine yourself ten years in the future. What kind of world do you want to live in?

A world brimming with innovation yet grounded in compassion?

How can you use your own skills and kindness to help create that future?

Close your eyes and let your imagination soar. Perhaps you see yourself as a doctor, using advanced technology to heal the sick. Maybe you envision yourself as a teacher, robots by your side, creating a more inclusive and engaging learning environment.

Write a short story or draw a picture depicting your vision for a positive future.

Remember, the future is not set in stone. With a combination of knowledge, kindness, and a dash of imagination, we can all contribute to building a better tomorrow.

Check Your Understanding

1. What milestone do the robots reach in this chapter?

The robots graduate from the A.I. Academy, marking the end of their formal education and the beginning of their journey into the world.

2. What message does Professor Lumi share with the graduates?

Professor Lumi likely emphasizes the potential of AI for positive change. She encourages the robots to use their knowledge and skills not just for technical advancements, but also to benefit humanity and create a better future.

3. How do the graduating robots express their aspirations?

The chapter might showcase some graduating robots sharing their dreams and goals for the future. These might involve using their skills in various ways, like Bolt using his strength for disaster relief, Chip employing his creativity in education, or Widget assisting in scientific research.

4. What is the overall tone of the chapter?

The chapter likely ends on a hopeful and optimistic note, emphasizing the potential for a harmonious future where humans and robots collaborate to build a better world.

5. What is the Actionable Activity asking you to do?

The Actionable Activity encourages you to use your imagination and consider the future. Imagine a world ten years from now and think about what kind of place you want it to be. Reflect on your own skills and kindness and brainstorm ways you can contribute to creating that positive future. This could be through writing a short story, drawing a picture, or simply starting a conversation about the future you envision.

Summary & Moral

Bolt Learns About Kindness: A Story about AI Friends

Bolt, a strong but new robot, goes to the A.I. Academy with other robots to learn about emotions, helping others, and using words carefully. He makes mistakes but learns from them.

Through fun activities and challenges, Bolt discovers that everyone has something special to offer and that kindness is the most important thing, no matter who you are!

Moral: Even robots can learn about kindness!

By helping others, using your words carefully, and understanding different perspectives, you can make the world a better place.

Thank You

Hey there reader!

Thanks for joining Bolt and his A.I. Academy friends on their adventure as a reader!

We hope you had a blast learning about kindness, teamwork, and the power of using your words and abilities for good.

Remember, just like Bolt, you have something special to offer the world. So be curious, be kind, and always strive to make a positive difference, one step (or roll) at a time!

Happy reading!

Regards

Rekha Kumari

[   ]

Don't miss out!

Visit the website below and you can sign up to receive emails whenever Rekha Kumari publishes a new book. There's no charge and no obligation.

https://books2read.com/r/B-A-QAJFB-QSOAD

BOOKS 2 READ

Connecting independent readers to independent writers.

Did you love *A.I. Academy: Where Robots Learn Kindness*? Then you should read *Grandma's Time Machine: An Adventure Through History*[1] by Rekha Kumari!

Is your bookshelf missing a dose of laughter, adventure, and a sprinkle of historical knowledge?

Look no further than **"Grandma's Time Machine: An Adventure Through History,"** a delightful tale that whisks you on a time-traveling journey unlike any other!

What makes this book a must-read for curious minds of all ages:

A Time-Travelingromp: Join Max and his Grandma on a series of wacky adventures through history. Their rickety time machine might land them in unexpected eras, but the mishaps lead to hilarious and unforgettable encounters! Imagine dodging a T-Rex in the Jurassic

---

1. https://books2read.com/u/mBnevk

2. https://books2read.com/u/mBnevk

Period (from a safe distance, of course!) or rocking out at a disco with Cleopatra!**Learning Made Fun:** Each chapter is like a portal to a different historical period. You'll discover fascinating facts about clothing, customs, and even brush shoulders with famous figures – all while having a blast with Max and Grandma's antics.**Activities Galore:** This book goes beyond just storytelling. Packed with interesting tidbits and engaging activities, it's a springboard for your own exploration of the past! Design your own time machine, create a comic strip depicting a day in medieval times, or research the life of a fascinating historical figure.**Perfect for All Ages:** "Grandma's Time Machine" is a delightful blend of humor, adventure, and historical intrigue. Whether you're a history buff or just starting to discover the wonders of different eras, this book has something for everyone.**Spark Curiosity and Imagination:** This book is more than just entertainment; it's an invitation to explore the past. By igniting a love for history, it can inspire young readers to delve deeper, ask questions, and discover the incredible stories waiting to be unearthed.

So, buckle up and get ready for a time-traveling adventure that will leave you laughing, learning, and maybe even a little inspired!

Also by Rekha Kumari

Grandma's Time Machine: An Adventure Through History
A.I. Academy: Where Robots Learn Kindness

About the Author

Rekha Kumari is a dynamic and accomplished individual, embodying the roles of both an expert entrepreneur and a passionate educator. With a wealth of experience in both fields, she has dedicated her life to empowering children and guiding them towards success.

As a seasoned entrepreneur, Rekha has navigated the complexities of the business world with finesse. Her innovative ideas, strategic vision, and unwavering determination have enabled her to establish herself as a leader in her industry. Through her ventures, she has not only achieved significant professional milestones but has also served as an inspiration to aspiring entrepreneurs, especially women, encouraging them to pursue their dreams fearlessly.

In addition to her entrepreneurial endeavors, Rekha is deeply committed to education and believes in the transformative power it holds. As a teacher, she goes beyond imparting knowledge; she nurtures young minds, instilling in them the values of resilience, determination, and excellence. Her teaching philosophy revolves around building strong foundations and fostering a growth mindset, equipping her students with the tools they need to become winners in life.

Rekha Kumari's unique blend of entrepreneurial acumen and educational expertise makes her a sought-after figure in both business and academic circles. Her dedication to empowering the next generation underscores her belief in the limitless potential of every child. Through her guidance and mentorship, she continues to shape future leaders and pave the way for a brighter tomorrow.